Warren's Journey

Warren's Journey

Michael Neal

iUniverse, Inc.
New York Lincoln Shanghai

Warren's Journey

iUniverse, Inc.

For information address:
iUniverse, Inc.
2021 Pine Lake Road, Suite 100
Lincoln, NE 68512
www.iuniverse.com

ISBN: 0-595-33862-3

Printed in the United States of America

Chapter 1

Warren stood up and looked out over the Lamar Valley in Yellowstone National Park. He was trying to find his pack. They had left earlier in the morning to go hunting. He wanted to find them and, hopefully, eat some of the fresh kill. He was hungry. Warren walked down into the valley and found new wolf tracks in the snow. He knew they were from his pack since no other packs hunted here.

Warren followed the tracks until he found a large, old elk. Everyone in his pack had eaten and was resting on a small ridge nearby. Warren walked over to the elk, which was now covered by ravens. He nudged several aside and started to eat.

"Who are you?" said one raven,

Warren looked up at the large black bird. "I am Warren. My father is the alpha male of the pack."

"I thought you might be his son. You look a lot like your father especially with the thick black fur."

Warren watched the raven eat. He was surprised how much a small animal, small compared to him, could eat. "Do you ever eat more than your stomach can handle?"

"Sometimes less, never more," said the raven. "Hi. My name is Ron. I want to ask you a question. I don't think I have ever seen you hunting with your pack. You look almost grown. You are not a pup anymore. Why don't you hunt?"

"You are right. I am not a pup. I am almost two years old. Anyway, hunting is a lot of work. You have to run a long distance and chase large prey. It is also dangerous. My uncle was hurt just last week when an elk kicked him in his ribs. It is easier to wait until the hunt is over and everyone is finished eating."

"I am surprised you don't have to help," said Ron.

"My parents are the alpha male and female and run the pack. I am also the largest of the young wolves." Warren stood up and raised his tail into the air with his head held high. "No one tells me what to do." Warren looked at Ron.

"You better do your share of the work," said Ron after a while. "I have been around wolf packs for years. I can tell you that it doesn't matter who your parents are if you don't do your share."

"Why don't you go bother someone else?" Warren said. "I am busy."

Ron flew away, and Warren ate until he was full. He walked over to the small ridge where his brothers and sisters were lying in the sun. Warren sat beside Tommy, his smallest brother.

"Where have you been?" Tommy asked.

"Waiting for you to fix breakfast." Warren laughed.

"Well, you should know that I helped bring down the elk today. Dad put me on the last leg of the chase, and I made the kill," Tommy said. He stood up and raised his tail as high as it would go.

The other young wolves laughed at Tommy. He dropped his tail and head and looked at the ground.

Warren stood up and growled at his smaller brother. "Big deal. You are lucky the elk didn't kick you in the head." Warren then nipped at Tommy's neck and growled again. Warren stood against his brother and raised his head, tail, and ears. Tommy lowered his tail and head. Warren was too big to fight.

"What is going on here?" Tommy and Warren turned to see their father standing close to them. "What are you doing Warren?" he asked.

"Oh, we are just playing, Dad," Warren said. Tommy did not say anything. No one said anything for a long time.

"Really Dad. We're just playing around."

"Maybe you should use your energy to help with our hunt. Tommy made the kill this morning. I am very proud of him. Where were you?"

"I was still asleep. Sorry. I will hunt next time," Warren said. Warren had dropped his tail and was looking down now.

"Warren, you have helped with your share of the work since you were born. You do not respect your brothers and sisters. You do not respect the pack. The pack has decided that you must leave. We do not want you here anymore."

Everyone looked up at their father. No one said anything. After a pause, Warren's father continued, "You must leave now. You cannot stay in the valley or hunt around here. Leave now." Warren's father stood up tall and close to Warren. Warren was not sure what to do.

"Where will I go? What will I do? How will I eat?" Warren asked. He was scared.

"You should have thought about that when you decided not to help your pack. Please leave now!"

Warren knew he had to leave. And he had to leave now. He looked at his father and his mother, who had walked up next to his father. He looked at his brothers and sisters. No one looked happy. Everyone just looked back at him.

Warren turned and walked away. After twenty feet, he put his tail between his legs and looked back at the pack. He hoped that he would be allowed back.

"Go on, Warren. You must leave," his father said. His mother did not say anything. Tommy looked at him and then looked away.

Warren turned and continued walking. He went to the top of a ridge where he hoped he could not be seen. He sat down and looked back where he had been. He could see his brothers and sisters playing. He did not know what the future would hold. At least for now, his stomach was full.

Ron flew up and landed on the ground next to Warren. "I told you so," said the raven. "You're in big trouble now. A young, lone wolf with no pack. Too bad."

"Go away and leave me alone. I will be fine," said Warren.

"All right. Go it alone. Good luck." Ron flew away. Warren sat and stared at the valley below the rest of the day.

Warren stood up and walked farther up the mountain. He sat where he could see the valley and watched the sun set. It began to snow before he found a place to sleep for the night.

A chorus of howling started from the valley. Warren liked howling and almost joined in as usual. He realized he should not since he was no longer in the pack, so he just lay by a tree and listened.

"What am I going to do?" he thought as he drifted off to sleep.

Chapter 2

Warren opened his eyes and looked around. He was cold. Nearly a foot of snow had fallen overnight. It took him a few minutes to fully wake up and remember what had happened. He sat up and tried to decide what to do next. Surely, his father would let him back in the pack. All he had to do was walk into the valley and say he was sorry. He would hunt and do his share of the work.

Warren stood up in the deep snow. He tried to walk, but it was difficult. He usually followed the pack in snow. His father led the way by making tracks for others to follow. He had not understood how hard it was to lead the way.

Warren managed to walk nearly half way down the hill before he became too tired to walk. He found a spot under a tree where the snow was not as deep and lay down to rest. He had nearly fallen asleep when he heard a noise. "It must be Dad coming to get me," he thought. He jumped up and started around the tree just in time to see his brother.

"Tommy? What are you doing here?" Warren said as his younger brother walked up to him. "Are you alone?" Warren looked behind Tommy for his father.

"Yes. I decided to leave the pack. It was only a matter of time before I was kicked out too. I thought we could team up and help each other out," Tommy said.

"Ha, ha," Warren laughed. "Help each other out! How can YOU help ME?"

"Hunting, for one thing. Look, we can help each other. Dad is not going to let you back in the pack. I heard Mom and him talking last night. I thought we could start our own pack."

Warren looked around at the deep snow. "Okay, you can start helping by leading me to a warmer valley. I never liked this place anyway."

"Okay," Tommy said as he turned and started walking though the deep snow. Warren followed in his tracks.

Warren and Tommy walked all day and did not stop until well after the sun had disappeared. They had not said much to each other throughout the day. The next day, they started walking again. Warren was quiet most of the morning.

Around noon, Tommy finally said, "Why are you so quiet Warren? I am not used to quiet around you." Tommy laughed a little.

Warren did not answer him. Nearly an hour later, Warren finally spoke, "Do you know where you are going?"

"Sure, you said you wanted a warmer place, so I am taking us out of the mountains."

"I hope you know what you're doing," Warren said. They traveled the rest of the day and late into the night. Both were tired when they found a patch of trees to settle into. Warren noticed that is was, indeed, warmer here.

The next morning, the two brothers started out again. Warren was still quiet. Tommy decided to let him be alone. He must be sad given what had happened.

After an hour of working through another narrow valley, Tommy stopped.

"What now? Why did you stop?" Warren asked. "Are you tired already?"

"No, but I see lunch," Tommy said.

Warren was starting to get hungry again. He looked through the trees and finally saw a deer. "A deer," he laughed. "That won't make a good lunch. I want elk. Or better yet, a bison calf. Let's not waste our time on a scraggly deer." Warren almost yelled the last sentence, and the deer jumped up and ran off.

Tommy turned around and ran at Warren. A shocked Warren pulled back a little then lunged at

Tommy. They fought for nearly a full minute. Warren was on top with Tommy's throat in his jaw. He stopped and jumped off of his brother.

"Never attack me," Warren said. "I am the big brother here."

"You won't be anything if you don't grow up and help me find food."

"What do you mean 'grow up,'" said Warren. "I'm much bigger than you."

"It doesn't matter how big you are if we don't work together. I know you never learned that in our pack. You never did your share."

"So if I am so lazy, and you don't like me, why did you follow me?" asked Warren.

"Well," said Tommy. "You are my big brother. I never said I didn't like you. You are lazy though."

"I like to pace myself," said Warren.

"Shhh, listen," Tommy said. "Can you hear that howling?"

Warren strained and was able to hear howling in the distance. "Yea I hear it. So what?" Warren sat down in the snow.

"We have to avoid that other pack. They'll kill us if they find us in their territory."

"Are you scared?" Warren said. He began to howl loudly. "Let them find us. Maybe we can share their hunt."

"Not likely," said Tommy. "I don't think it's smart of you to howl and let them know we're here."

Warren howled again and then laughed. Suddenly, Tommy and Warren were surrounded by several wolves. Tommy put his tail between his legs and lowered his head. He wanted to show he knew who was in charge. Warren stood tall and raised his ears.

The pack moved closer to the two brothers. A large male walked to Warren and stood over him with his tail raised high. Warren was getting nervous. This wolf did not seem happy to see him.

"Hello, I'm Warren," he said. "This is my brother Tommy. Do you have food? We are hungry."

The large male wolf laughed, "We have food now." He smiled and looked at the other wolves. Warren did not understand. He looked over at Tommy.

Tommy whispered, "I think he means we're his food. Run!"

Warren and Tommy started running as fast as they could. The large male followed Warren and caught him quickly. He started to bite Warren when Tommy jumped on him from the side.

Warren was free, and he jumped up. He saw two wolves jump on Tommy before he began running again. He did not stop for a long time. When he finally did, he lay down, exhausted. After he had caught his breath, he sat up and looked around. It was then that he realized Tommy was not there.

Chapter 3

Warren did not know what to do. Tommy had not followed him. Should he go back to find him? He started to walk slowly back. However, he stopped after only a few hundred yards, and he turned around and began to run again. He ran until he was too tired to run any more, which is a long distance for a wolf. He finally lay down under a tree to rest and fell asleep.

The afternoon sun kept Warren warm and asleep until late into the day. He awoke as the sun began to set and realized he was very hungry. As Warren sat listening to his stomach growl, he wondered how he could find some food. He was deep in thought when a large black object suddenly landed by his head.

"Hello Warren," said Ron. "It's been an interesting few days for you."

"How did you find me?" asked Warren.

"I have been following you since you were kicked out of your pack."

"Did you see what happened to Tommy?" Warren asked.

"No," said Ron. "I followed you. I'm not sure what happened to him. Do you really care anyway?"

Warren looked away at the distant mountains. He did not answer Ron.

After a long silence, Ron finally said, "So I'd guess you are getting hungry. Three to four days without food is a long time for a young, growing wolf like you. What are you going to do for food?"

Warren did not say anything. He continued to stare at the mountains.

"Well," said Ron, "I know where you can find food. Already killed, just like you like it." He laughed.

"Where is food?" asked Warren. He needed to eat even if it meant talking to this bird.

"Follow me, and I will show you. There is only one slight issue. But I will tell you that after you have had your fill."

Warren was not sure what Ron meant. He wondered if Tommy was going to show up. He stood up and said, "All right, bird. Take me to your secret stash of food." Warren cast a quick look back as they walked off just in case Tommy was coming.

Ron flew up into the sky and circled for a few minutes. Warren could not see what he was doing, but waited for him to go in one direction. Warren was growing impatient. Finally Ron swooped down and yelled, "Follow me."

Warren had to run to keep up with Ron. He had not realized ravens could fly so fast. After several minutes, Warren smelled an elk. He started running faster and came to a river bed. He ran down it and into a huge grizzly bear. The bear was angry to be disturbed as it ate the elk. It turned around and took a swipe at Warren who had fallen down. Warren pulled back just in time and quickly ran back up the river bank. Ron landed next to him.

"That was not funny. What are you trying to do, get me killed?" said Warren.

"No, I am trying to get you fed. Then maybe you won't be so cranky."

"How can I eat when that bear is there?" asked Warren.

"You wait your turn. We ravens always have to wait until you big guys are finished eating. Have a little patience, my friend."

"Okay. I guess I can wait. How much does a bear eat, anyway?"

"As much as he wants," laughed Ron. Warren did not laugh. He lay down and watched the bear eat. The elk looked good. It was nice for Ron to help him find it.

Warren continued to watch the bear eat for a long time. He wondered what his old pack was doing. He wondered if Tommy was okay.

"How you boys doing?" said a voice from behind Warren. He jumped up and turned around to see a large grey wolf walking up close to him. The wolf was standing tall and proud. "Or should I say what are you boys doing?"

"We are waiting for the bear to leave. What do you think we're doing?" Ron said quickly. Warren thought Ron was disrespectful. He would not be to this large intruder.

"Why are you waiting for the bear to leave? You can't catch your own food?" The wolf looked at Warren.

"Sure I can," said Warren. "I am just resting here, and this stupid bird landed and started bothering me." He glared at Ron.

"Yea, right. I'm bothering you," Ron said. He flew off.

"Ravens can be bothersome," said the grey wolf. "My name is Jack."

"I'm Warren."

"Are you in a pack, Warren?"

"No, I left my pack recently. It was boring."

"Boring to be in your own pack? That's funny. It is easier to eat when you have friends helping hunt," said Jack.

Warren did not say anything.

"You don't have to follow bears around and wait around like a coyote for scraps," said Jack. "I would never eat someone else's kill." Jack raised his tail high and pushed his nose in the air.

"I am not a coyote. I was just going to hunt, as a matter of fact," said Warren, insulted. "If you want, we could hunt together."

"You know, I could use a partner. Do you want to be in Jack's Pack?"

"Sure. Who else is in your pack?" asked Warren.

"Well, it is just you and me for now," said Jack. "Do we need anyone else?"

"No, I guess not," said Warren. "Is this our territory?"

"Nope. We have a huge territory not far from here. The hunting is great, and it is easier than elk and bison hunting."

Warren did not know what Jack meant. He did not care. He was too excited to be in a new pack.

"Let's go," said Jack. "I'm hungry. I want to see how good a hunter you are Warren."

The two wolves headed off together. Warren looked back just in time to see the bear finish eating. He saw a coyote and several ravens move in as soon as the bear left. The kill looked good. He wondered if he could eat some. He was really hungry. He looked at Jack walking quickly away and decided to stay with him. He wondered what adventures were ahead. He wondered what was so easy to hunt in Jack's Pack's territory.

Chapter 4

Warren followed Jack for the rest of the day and long into the night. They came to the top of a mountain pass and Jack stopped. "Let's sleep here tonight," he said.

"How much farther to your territory?" asked Warren.

"Not far. We can make it by the end of the day tomorrow," said Jack.

Warren settled down on a patch of grass and fell asleep immediately. The next thing he knew there was an odd pecking on his nose. He opened his eyes and saw Ron only three inches from his face. Warren jumped.

"Sorry wolf boy. I didn't mean to scare you," Ron laughed.

"Who are you calling names? Better watch out bird brain. I might have you for breakfast," said Warren. He was not happy to see the raven. Warren looked around, but he did not see Jack. He worried that Jack had left him.

"Don't worry. Jack is just over there on the ridge. He didn't leave you. He would not leave his latest protégé."

"What do you mean?" asked Warren.

"Jack is always coming around here looking for young wolves to join his pack. Once he finds one, they head off to the human's valley. A few months later, Jack is back looking for someone new."

"What? Looking for someone new? The human's valley? What are you saying, Ron?"

"Oh, so now you are interested in wise old Ron's knowledge," said the raven. He jumped up on a log and looked around. Ron spoke again. This time he lowered his voice. "Well, you should be. Jack is a bad wolf. He is not someone you should hang around. He hunts human's animals. He makes his pack do all the dangerous work, and then he eats the kills. There have been three or four young wolves like you head off with Jack who didn't return."

"What happened to them?" asked Warren. He was worried.

"The humans got them. The humans kill any wolf that kills their animals. You should stay here and learn to hunt elk, deer, and bison like most wolves. Don't go off with the likes of Jack."

Ron suddenly flew off. Warren turned around and saw Jack coming down the ridge toward him.

"Good morning Warren," Jack said as he walked up. "I see you like to sleep late. That's okay in Jack's Pack, as long as you can hunt."

"Jack," Warren said, "yesterday you said that hunting in your territory was easier than hunting elk and bison. What do you hunt?"

"Why do you ask?" said Jack. "That silly raven been talking to you?"

"No. Well, yes. He said you hunt human's animals. Isn't that dangerous?"

"No," said Jack. "It is easy to hunt those animals. They are slow. Many times, they are even inside fences and cannot get away. It is easy hunting. It's Jack's Pack hunting."

Warren was not sure what to say. Jack seemed to know what he was talking about. Warren said, "Ron, I mean that raven, also said that many wolves like me join Jack's Pack and don't come back."

Jack looked at Warren's face then said, "Are you going to listen to that bird or me? I am offering you a once in a lifetime opportunity to be in the number one pack. It's time to go. Do you want to come with me or not?"

Warren thought for a minute. Was Ron right? Would Jack get him into trouble? He was not sure. He was sure he was hungry. "I want to come with you. Let's go."

Jack led Warren at a fast pace through light snow for the rest of the day. As the sun was about to set, they reached the top of another mountain pass.

"See that valley down there?" Jack motioned to Warren. "That is our territory. I like to stay between here and there when I'm not hunting. It is peaceful. There are no other wolves here to bother us. Did I tell you that? There are also no bears to steal our kill. And there are not many, if any, ravens around to bother us. This is a really quiet place."

"Sounds good," said Warren. "But, don't you miss other wolves? Don't we need a female for our pack?"

Jack was quiet. It was the first time he did not have an answer for a question. He just started walking down the mountain. Warren followed quietly. It was dark by the time they were most of the way down the mountain. Warren was ready to go to sleep.

"Hey Warren. Let's go on our first hunt," said Jack.

"Now?" said Warren. "I'm tired. We have been walking for two days straight."

"I'm hungry. Let's go hunt. First, I need to tell you the rules for Jack's Pack hunts. We have two types of food here: sheep and cattle. The sheep are easier to catch, especially the lambs. The cows are a little harder, but they have a lot of meat on them."

Warren listened closely. Jack continued, "I will take the lead and find the one to kill. You follow behind me then take over when I separate the animal from its herd. Just like you did when hunting in your old pack. Right?"

"Right," Warren said. He was not going to tell Jack he had never made a kill. They started down into the valley. A full moon was out, and it was almost as light as day. Jack was in the lead and moving slowly and quietly toward the herd of sheep.

"One more thing," said Jack as they reached the tree line, "If you see bright lights or hear loud banging sounds, run as fast as you can back up the mountain. I will meet you there."

Warren wanted to ask what that meant, but Jack jumped out of the trees and started chasing the sheep. Warren followed as best he could. He wanted to impress Jack on their first hunt.

Warren was getting excited. Jack ran right and then left. He was fast and quick on his turns. Warren kept up with him and then saw a single, small sheep turn away from the herd. Warren ran as fast as he could to the sheep. Although he had never made a kill, he knew what to do and sank his teeth deep into the sheep's neck. He bit as hard as he could. The sheep stopped running and fell down. Warren had made his first kill.

"Nice job," Jack said as he ran up. "You must have been a good hunter in your old pack. Let's eat quickly." The two wolves ate in silence until they were full. Jack led the way back into the trees and up the hill. They both stretched out on a ridge-line. Warren was still excited from the hunt and his stomach was full. He felt happy for the first time since Tommy disappeared.

Chapter 5

Warren and Jack traveled and hunted together through the remaining winter months, through spring, summer, and into the fall. The territory for Jack's Pack was actually anywhere they could find food. Warren remained uneasy about hunting human's food and was even able to convince Jack to hunt deer and elk a few times. Warren had become a very good hunter.

One cold fall day, Warren and Jack walked up a tall mountain pass and looked down into the valley below. It was Warren's old home, the Lamar Valley. Warren stopped walking.

"Hey buddy, what's the matter," Jack asked.

"This is my old home. I don't want to go down there," said Warren.

"Why not?" asked Jack. "You could say hello to your parents." Jack started to walk down.

"No I can't," said Warren. He turned and began to walk the other way. He did not notice, or even care, what Jack did. Warren walked for hours and went over the pass and down into another valley and lay down. He was alone.

Warren watched the sun drop out of the sky. He wondered what his mother and father were doing. He wondered if Tommy was alive.

As the moon rose in the clear sky, Warren stood up, leaned back and began to howl. He had only howled a few times in the past year. Jack was wary of being noticed and did not like to howl. But tonight, Warren did not care. He was lonely. Warren howled for a long time. He felt better when he finished and lay back on the ground.

"What do you think you are doing?" said a voice from behind a tree. Warren looked up and saw Jack running toward him. "Why are you making so much noise? You know we are surrounded by other, larger packs."

"So what, I don't care anymore," said Warren.

"You better care. Let's get out of here," said Jack.

"And go where?" said Warren.

"Let's go find a tasty sheep," said Jack.

"Not another sheep. That is a lazy wolf's food."

"Who are you calling lazy? Sheep was fine for you when I found you fighting ravens for bear left-overs. Now that is lazy." Warren growled at Jack and nipped at his ear. Jack jumped at Warren and bit his nose hard. "Don't push your luck or you will be back to stealing food like a mangy coyote."

Warren was angry, but he knew Jack was right. It was much easier to hunt food in a pack. He did not say anything. Jack started walking off and Warren followed at a distance. They walked all night. As the sun rose, Warren could see the sheep herd where he had made his first kill. He also noticed he was hungry. It had been a while since he had eaten.

Jack started down toward the fence. Suddenly, he stopped and started running back up the hill. He ran right by Warren but did not say anything. Warren heard a loud bang and saw a stick next to Jack fly up into the air. He did not know what to do. Jack was now out of sight. Warren heard another bang and some dirt next to him flew up and into his face. He was scared and began to run.

Warren heard yet another bang and felt a sharp pain in his back leg. He kept running even though his leg hurt. He ran and ran until he came around a large tree and almost ran over Jack.

"Good, you made it," said Jack calmly.

"What was that?" asked Warren. He could barely breathe.

"The humans don't like it when we eat their animals. Sometimes they express their dislike a little more forcefully."

"This has happened before? Why didn't you warn me? They hurt me!" Warren showed Jack his back leg. It was bleeding.

"Warn you about what? This is safer than hunting elk and bison. This is the first time we have been attacked in a year."

"But it is not the first time you have been attacked. Ron was right. There have been wolves killed in Jack's Pack." Warren fell down as the pain in his leg became more intense.

"Yea, so what. Some slow wolves didn't make it. But you did. What's the big deal."

"Look at my leg," Warren yelped. "It hurts."

"It's just a scratch. Quit crying and let's get out of here." Jack stood up and began walking off. Warren had the feeling he better follow him or he would be left alone. Maybe he shouldn't follow. Warren was not sure what to do.

After a few minutes, Warren stood up and limped off where Jack had walked.

It took several weeks for Warren's leg to heal. Jack shared his kills with Warren during this time. They had found a sick old moose by accident one afternoon that fed them for several days.

"Jack," Warren said one afternoon. "Let's go into the forest and only hunt elk from now on. Let's not go after human's food anymore."

"And just where do you want us to go?" said Jack. "There are packs everywhere. They will kill us if we move into their territory. Besides, I like sheep and cattle. It's easy hunting and easy living. You don't have to work as hard. I like it."

"But it isn't safe," said Warren. "It is also strange to hunt these animals. We should be hunting elk and bison and deer. And we need a female in our pack."

Jack did not say anything. Warren became quiet as well.

"Warren," said Jack. "We made it through the long, cold winter. We have had only one case where we were bothered. I think we are doing all right. Is your leg good enough to travel? I want to head off to the cattle ranch today. We will need to eat in a few days, and I am hungry for cow."

Warren did not say anything. He knew this was not right, but he knew he had to eat and survive. He decided to follow Jack. What else could he do?

It took the two wolves several days to reach Jack's favorite ranch. They were both hungry by then. Jack ran out to the field where the cows were grazing. The snow had completely melted in this valley, and it was actually warm. Warren followed Jack toward the cows. He was nervous.

Suddenly, Jack jumped up and started to chase the herd. Warren started to follow him when he heard a bang. The humans were there. Warren froze. He did not move an inch. He could see Jack turn and begin to run back. He was nearly back to Warren when another bang rang out, and Jack fell.

Warren was only fifty feet away from Jack and did not know what to do. Should he go help Jack? Should he run? He heard the humans and another bang. A twig next to him flew up. Warren jerked away and began running as fast as he could. He ran for hours until he collapsed deep in the forest. He was tired, but he was okay.

Chapter 6

"Well look whose back in the valley." Warren opened his eyes and saw Ron sitting next to him. "I wondered if you would ever make your way back here. Where is Jack?"

"He didn't make it," Warren said. Ron looked surprised. Warren did not say anything else.

"I told you not to hang out with him," Ron said after a while. Warren still did not say anything.

"Have you decided to find a pack and settle down?" asked Ron.

"Quit bugging me. I mean, you aren't exactly a social bird either. Why aren't you in a pack, I mean flock, or whatever ravens fly in?" Warren asked.

"Well," Ron said, "ravens are always fighting for the scraps you wolves leave behind. I am tired of the whole thing. It is too much work and not enough working together. It's a dog eat dog world out there." Looking at Warren, he added, "I know that statement has a different meaning to wolves."

Warren started laughing and looked over at Ron. Maybe he liked this old bird after all.

"You look quite a bit bigger. I guess I can't really call you wolf boy anymore," said Ron. "Did you finally learn to hunt?"

"I did, and I'm pretty good too," said Warren.

"Hum," said Ron. "Maybe we can make a deal. I will find prey for us. You kill it, and we both eat it."

"I know the food you like. Bear scraps. No thanks," said Warren. "I prefer to hunt my own food."

"That's what I mean. For example, there is a coyote only a few hundred feet from here. He would make a good snack for a big wolf like you." Ron flew up into the air and began to circle. Warren was hungry, and he did not like coyotes, especially if they were in his territory.

Warren followed Ron and found the coyote stalking a marmot. Warren chased the coyote away and killed the marmot. He and Ron shared the meal. Afterwards, Warren said, "Maybe we can work together. I always thought you ravens were a pain, but if you find food I can hunt, we can be partners."

"I agree," said Ron.

The two friends spent the spring and summer helping each other. When hunting was poor, Warren followed Ron to other kills or old, dead animals. Although Warren preferred hunting, hunger always won out. No matter how sparse the meals were, he never considered going back to the human's valley. He felt lucky to have escaped.

The first snowfall of the winter was earlier than usual. Warren was walking through the valley the next afternoon when he came upon another wolf. She was a large, grey female and alone. The female saw him and stopped.

"What do you want?" she asked.

"Nothing. Just exploring. My name is Warren."

"My name is Marie. Are you alone Warren?" Marie asked.

"Yes, are you?"

"Yes I am. I left my pack a few days ago." Marie looked at Warren a long time. "You are a big wolf Warren. Why aren't you in a pack?"

"I was until recently. I am starting my own pack now," Warren quickly said. He stood tall and proud. "You can join me if you want."

Marie walked around Warren several times. "How good a hunter are you?" she asked.

"Why don't you find out? Let's go hunt, and I will show you." The two wolves started down toward a river in a meadow. There did not appear to be any prey around. Warren stopped near a small tree. Ron flew up and landed on it.

"Who's your girlfriend, Warren?" he asked.

"She is not my girlfriend," said Warren. "Marie and I are going to hunt together. If it works out, we will form our pack. Is that okay with you?"

Marie looked at Warren and turned her head sideways. "Are you friends with this raven?" she asked.

"Well, sort-of," said Warren. He looked up at Ron. "Well, yes I am. Ron is a good spotter for prey. We work together." Warren looked at Marie. He could not tell what she was thinking.

"A raven leading the hunt. This should be interesting," Marie said. "Show me what ya got, big bird."

Warren was relieved. He was worried Marie would make fun of him for working with a raven. She seemed like she could become a good friend.

Ron took off and flew away. Marie and Warren walked up to a ridgeline to look around. They did not see any prey and stretched out near the tree line. Warren had nearly fallen asleep when three small wolf pups ran by him. They were playing and did not pay much attention to Marie or him.

Warren stood up and started walking toward the pups. Suddenly, another wolf jumped on him and began to bite his back. Warren reacted and turned to fight the other wolf. Warren flipped the wolf over onto its back and jumped on top. He started to bite the wolf's neck but stopped.

"Tommy? Tommy? Is that you?" Warren said. He hopped off his brother.

"Warren, is it really you?" The two brothers jumped around with joy at seeing each other again.

"I thought you were dead," said Warren. "I mean, I ran off and left you." Warren dropped his head. "I'm sorry Tommy."

"It's okay brother. I managed to get away. But I could not find you. I looked for you for weeks and finally gave up. Then I met Ally."

Warren perked up. "Who is Ally?" he asked.

"My mate. We formed our own pack. These pups are ours." Tommy howled. Warren heard another wolf howl a short distance away. "She will be here in a minute. You are in our territory."

Marie walked over to the two wolves. "Aren't you going to introduce me?" she asked Warren.

"Tommy, this is Marie, my new friend. Marie, this is Tommy, my brother."

"Nice to meet you, Tommy," said Marie just as a large female wolf came running up to them.

"And Marie and Warren, this is Ally."

The four adult wolves stood around and talked for over an hour as the pups played nearby. Warren told Tommy about Jack's Pack and his adventures with the humans. Marie listened closely to Warren's stories. Tommy told Warren about his new pack and the excitement of becoming a father.

The day was ending and night ready to start. A chorus of howls started in the distance. Warren looked at Tommy.

"I know what you're thinking, Warren, but this is our territory," said Tommy. Ally looked uneasy.

"Then what is all that noise?" said Warren.

"This small pack thinks they can move in here because the hunting is good and take over. I have fought them twice already."

"And nearly been killed," added Ally. "There are three males and two females in that pack. She looked at Tommy. "So we may have to move somewhere else."

"Or maybe not. What if we joined you guys?" asked Marie. Warren and Tommy looked at each other.

"Warren, let's go over there and talk," said Tommy.

Warren followed Tommy to a small clump of bushes.

"Look brother," said Tommy. "I don't want you in my pack. I'm happy. I would hate to fight you to see who becomes the alpha male. I wouldn't want to hurt my own brother." Tommy made a short laugh. "Besides, I know I can't trust you. If things get tough, you will just run away. Again."

Warren looked at his brother. He knew he would not run away. But he understood why Tommy felt that way. He also knew he could easily beat him in a fight. "Look," said Warren, "We are just passing through. Marie and I are going to start our own pack several valleys from here. Okay?"

Tommy looked relieved. The brothers walked back to the females. "Warren and Marie have to be moving on," said Tommy. Marie looked at Warren. Warren looked away.

"Let's go Marie. We have a long way to go. Bye Tommy."

Warren and Marie started walking. They went over one ridge and stretched out for the night. Warren had a bad feeling about his brother.

Chapter 7

"I don't understand why you don't want his help. He is a large wolf. He could help us," said Ally. The pups were asleep.

"You don't know anything about my brother. He was thrown out of our pack for being lazy. I followed him to start a pack." Tommy stopped talking.

"So, what happened?" asked Ally.

"We were playing around one day, and Warren started howling. I told him to be quiet, that there were other wolves around. He laughed and kept howling. Then a pack appeared, and they attacked us. Attacked me! Warren ran off and left me there. I barely escaped. I was hurt badly."

"Wow. You never told me that before."

"I was, I mean, I am ashamed of my brother. Sure he is big and strong. But he is lazy and not brave at all. We couldn't depend on him."

Wolves started howling nearby. Ally and Tommy looked at each other. They did not talk anymore that night. Ally eventually fell asleep, but Tommy stayed awake the rest of the night.

One ridge over, Warren listened to the howling. He was worried about his brother and his new family. He knew Tommy would never trust him. Warren lay awake and stared at the stars until morning.

As the sun began to rise, Warren stood up and looked around. It was an overcast and cool morning. Marie was still asleep, and Ron was sitting on the rock beside Marie.

"Hello," said Ron. "What are you guys doing over here?" Marie was awake now.

"We are looking for our own territory," said Marie.

"Do you know whose territory this is?" asked Ron. "Someone you know."

"Yes. It's Tommy's. We talked with him yesterday," said Warren.

"Did he talk to you?" asked Ron.

"Yes, of course. We're brothers." Warren looked at the raven.

"Just wondering. I wasn't sure what he would say. Did he tell you he is fighting for his territory?"

"Yes, he did," said Marie. "Warren, is this bird always so nosy?"

Ron and Warren looked at each other and laughed.

"Yes he is," said Warren. "But he's okay."

"Warren, the territory fight Tommy is planning is not a good idea. The other pack is strong. I have seen them fight. They don't lose."

"Why are you telling me this? We are leaving soon. That fight is Tommy's fight." Warren looked at Marie. She looked away. He looked at Ron. Ron looked away too.

"What? What do you want me to do? Tommy wants me to leave. He's the one who wants us to leave. He will be all right."

"Just like before?" said Ron. "He was almost killed. He has young pups now. And a mate. He needs help."

Warren looked at the thickening mist. He knew Ron was right. But should he, could he, help Tommy? He did not know.

Suddenly, howling started from close by. It was not Tommy, or Ally. Warren and Marie ran up to the ridge. They saw several adult wolves running towards Tommy and Ally.

Warren looked at Marie. "Stay here," he said. He then ran after the wolves. Marie ran behind him.

Warren was a strong and fast runner. He nearly caught the wolves before they came upon Tommy and his family. Warren stopped short and watched.

"Hey, little wolf. We told you to get out of our territory," said the largest male. "Since you are still here, you and your pack will have to pay the consequences."

Tommy and Ally moved in front of the pups. "This is our territory," said Tommy. "We were here first."

The three intruders looked at each other and smiled. "Maybe, but we will be here last," said the large female. The two males ran and jumped on Tommy. The female took on Ally. The pups ran off.

Warren watched the fighting for a few seconds. It was clear Tommy and Ally could not win.

"What are you doing?" said Marie as she ran up. "Go help him." She ran down and started helping Ally fight the other female. Warren ran to the two males and jumped on the largest one who had Tommy by the throat. He knocked him off Tommy. The second male knocked Tommy down then ran to attack Warren.

The wolves fought ferociously. Warren was knocked down and rolled against a tree. Tommy looked at him. Warren jumped up and ran into the woods. The two males then turned to Tommy and began to attack him again. Tommy fought bravely and even managed to hurt one of the males.

The largest male, however, jumped on Tommy and pushed him down. Just then, Warren jumped from the trees and knocked the male off Tommy. Warren fought like he had never fought before. He pinned the large male down and could have killed him, but he stopped.

Twenty feet away, Ally and Marie held the female down. They had hurt her enough that she was out of the fight.

Tommy had won his fight too. The three beaten wolves got up and gathered away from Tommy.

"I suggest you leave," said Tommy. "As I said, this is our territory. If you come back, we will kill you." The three wolves lowered their heads and ran off.

Warren stood and watched the intruders until they were out of sight. He ran back over to Tommy and Ally. They were all right. The pups were there too. Marie had a small injury but was okay.

"Warren, where did you come from?" Tommy asked. "I thought for sure you had run away again."

"I would not leave my brother," said Warren. He stood tall and proud.

"Why don't you and Marie stay and join our pack?" said Tommy. "You've earned it."

"Sorry brother. We want to start our own pack. Anyway, I would hate to fight you for alpha." Warren winked at Tommy.

Warren and Marie walked up to the ridge line. Warren stopped and looked back at his little brother and his family one last time. He could not help himself and broke out in a loud and piercing howl. Tommy and his family answered back before Warren smiled and headed toward another valley.

Visit www.Courageouscritters.com

0-595-33862-3

Printed in the United States
78231LV00005B/847-870

9 780595 338627